LEVEL 2 READER

Pet Charms

The Lost Pony

by Amy Edgar
illustrated by Jomike Tejido

SCHOLASTIC INC.

For my daughters, Sophia and Fuji

ISBN 978-1-338-30264-6

10 9 8 7 6 5 4 3 2 1   18 19 20 21 22

Printed in Jiaxing City, China   68
First printing 2018

Book design by Two Red Shoes Design

Molly had a magic bracelet.

When she wore it, she could understand animals.

No one knew her secret.

Molly was packing to spend the night at her friend Lexie's house.

Molly lived next door to her best friend, Lexie. The first snow of winter was on its way. The friends had planned a sleepover full of snowy fun.

Lexie opened the door in her warmest slippers.
"Hey, Molly," said Lexie. "I'm glad you're here."
"Me, too," said Molly. "It feels like it could start
snowing any time."

Molly went over to Chocolate and Vanilla to say hello. The two bunnies had been Lexie's birthday surprise. Molly started to talk to the bunnies, but she looked down to see her bracelet was missing.
Without it, she would not be able to understand what they said.

"Oh, no!" said Molly. "I've lost my bracelet again!"
"I'll help you find it," said Lexie. "What did you do yesterday?"

"I visited the new pony at the stable with Aunt Vera," said Molly.

"I love ponies!" said Lexie. "Maybe your bracelet is there? Let's go look for it and see the pony, too."

They bundled up and headed out into the cold.
A puppy named Mr. Wiggles ran out of the stable
to greet them.
Molly had saved the puppy during a rainstorm.
He had given her the magic bracelet.

Molly hugged Mr. Wiggles and followed him inside. "Aunt Vera," said Molly. "Lexie wants to meet the new pony."

"Hi, girls," she said. "I have bad news. A snowstorm is coming, and the pony is missing."

"Oh no!" cried the girls.

"What happened?" asked Molly.

"I'm not sure," said Aunt Vera, "but I think she ran away."

Lexie saw something sparkly in the pony's stall.
"I found your bracelet!" shouted Lexie.
"You are the best!" said Molly. "I must have
taken it off to groom the pony."

"Hey, are these funny shoes for the pony?" asked Lexie.

"Yes," said Aunt Vera. "The farrier is coming today."

"What's a farrier?" asked Molly.

"A farrier puts on horseshoes," said Aunt Vera. "These will help keep the pony's feet safe in the snow and ice."

"Then we better find her before the storm," said Lexie.

"Let's go!" said Molly, putting on her bracelet. She remembered how much the pony liked carrots. So she put some in her pocket.

Aunt Vera went one way to look for the pony.
The girls went another.

They called for the pony as they walked down the road.

"This pony needs a good name," said Lexie.

"We'll have to think of one," said Molly.

"Why do you think she ran away?" asked Lexie.
"I don't know," said Molly. "Since she was new,
maybe she didn't know that Aunt Vera takes
great care of all animals."

Finally, they heard a sound in the woods nearby.

"It's the pony!" shouted Lexie.

"Let's talk softly," whispered Molly. "She looks scared."

Molly took the carrots out of her pocket.

The girls walked slowly toward the pony.
At first, the pony snorted and stamped.
Then Molly showed her the carrots.
"I think she remembers you," said Lexie.
"Plus she loves carrots!" added Molly.

"Wow, she is so beautiful!" said Lexie.
Molly was wearing her bracelet.
So she heard the pony say, "Thank you."
The girls petted her neck and mane while she ate the carrots.

Molly whispered in the pony's ear. "Why did you run away?"

The pony neighed, "I heard a storm was coming, and I did not like it when they took off my shoes."

Molly told her, "A storm is just a bunch of snowflakes, and Aunt Vera has new snowshoes to keep your feet safe in the snow."

"Oh," neighed the pony. "I was scared, but now I understand."

"Look! The first snowflakes are falling," said Lexie.

"Hey," said Molly, "Snowflake is a perfect pony name. Plus, the white spots on her nose kind of look like snowflakes."

The pony agreed with a whinny.

"We can still beat the storm," said Lexie.
"Yes," said Molly, "let's go."
She whispered to Snowflake, "You are safe with us.
Plus, I know where to find more carrots."
Snowflake tossed her mane and followed.

The girls led Snowflake safely back to the stable.
The ground was covered with snow.
Aunt Vera was thrilled to see them all.
Snowflake nuzzled Aunt Vera as she added fresh
hay to the stall.

Goodbye, Snowflake," said the girls.

The name fits," said Aunt Vera.

Thank you for helping me, Molly," whinnied Snowflake.

Sure, see you soon!" called Molly.

I can't wait to see her in her new snowshoes,"

aid Lexie.

Molly bent down to tell Mr. Wiggles goodbye.
"Nice work, Molly," said Mr. Wiggles.
"Thanks!" Molly said with another hug.

Lexie and Molly ran all the way home.

They opened their mouths to catch snowflakes.

"Tomorrow, we could build a snowman," said Lexie.

"Or go sledding," added Molly.

Inside, they drank hot cocoa and watched a funny movie. They held Chocolate and Vanilla and petted their soft fur. When the girls looked outside, they saw even more fluffy white snow.

Soon, it was time to snuggle into their warm
sleeping bags. Before Molly fell asleep, she
saw her bracelet sparkle brightly. She blinked.
A new pony charm was hanging from it!

"This has been the best snowy sleepover ever," said Lexie.

"It sure has," said Molly. "We made another new animal friend."

Then she smiled again.
She was thinking about Snowflake with
her new shoes, safe and snug in the stable.

"Good night, Lexie," said Molly.
"Good night, Molly," said Lexie.
They fell asleep, dreaming of the snowy
fun they would have the next day.